The Time Machine

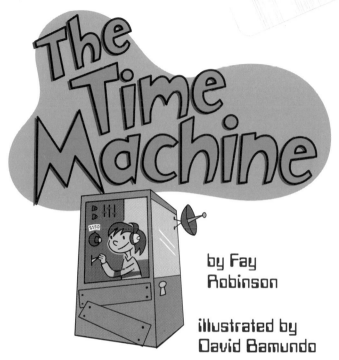

by Fay
Robinson

illustrated by
David Bamundo

Scott Foresman

Editorial Offices: Glenview, Illinois • New York, New York
Sales Offices: Reading, Massachusetts • Duluth, Georgia
Glenview, Illinois • Carrollton, Texas • Menlo Park, California

It all began when I asked what we were having for dinner.

"Broccoli pie," said my dad. "Yum!"

"We never get to eat what I want!" I said.

"And what would that be?" asked my dad.

"Burgers and fries—every night."

"That wouldn't be good for you," said Dad.

"Yes, it would," I said.

"Respect your parents," said my mom.

She always says that.

I decided to go to Daniel's. He lives down the street.

"First you must practice the piano and do your homework," Mom said. "And you need to comb your hair!" She always says that too.

"I never get to do what I want!" I said.

"Respect your parents," said my mom. Humph!

I practiced the piano. Then I went to my room to do my homework.

My sister Cindy had spilled nail polish all over my desk—again!

It was time for a new life!
I finished my homework.
"I'm going to Daniel's!" I yelled.
"Be back by dinner time," said
my mom.
"Maybe," I said.
Guess what she said.

I zipped over to Daniel's on my bike.
It used to be Cindy's bike. Her old pink
hand-me-down. Yuck!

When I arrived at Daniel's, I said,
"Today's the day."

"But we haven't tested it!" he said. We
were talking about our time machine.

"I'll test it now. I can't wait another
second!" I said.

I set the machine for the year 2150. Then I turned it on. I didn't even wait long enough to get scared. I was ready for some excitement!

ZIP, ZAP, CLANK!

I blinked. The next thing I knew I had arrived . . . somewhere. I opened the door slowly.

A face greeted me. "My name is Neo," he said. He looked like an ordinary boy—sort of.

"Cool name!" I said. "I'm Jenny."

"I've never heard of that name," he said. Wow!

"I bet no one ever tells you to comb your hair," I said.

"Well, no," said Neo.

"Where did you come from?"
Neo asked.

I explained everything. "I need a new life," I said. "I'm ready for excitement."

"Well, why don't you come over for dinner?" said Neo.

"What are you having?" I asked.

"Burgers and fries," he said.
Perfect!

"Get on my sky bike," said Neo.
I couldn't believe it. The future
was great!

I met Neo's parents. We sat down for dinner. Then I spied a clump of something strange on my plate.

"Excuse me," I said politely. "Aren't we having burgers and fries?"

"Yes!" said Neo's mom. "Burgers, fries, and vitamins. We blend all our meals. It saves so much time!"

Suddenly I wasn't hungry.

Then Neo's dad said, "Neo, it's time to practice the pian-accord-a-horn."

"Do I have to?" whined Neo.

"Respect your parents," said Neo's mom.

Neo practiced his music. It sounded really hard to play.

When he was finished, he turned on his computer. I spied over his shoulder. Strange letters and numbers filled the screen.

"What are you doing?" I asked.

"Homework," he said.

Yikes!

Suddenly I was hungry for broccoli. Homework didn't seem so bad. I couldn't wait to play the piano. I even missed my parents.

"I have to go," I said. "Thanks for dinner! Come visit sometime!"

"Maybe I will," said Neo.

ZIP, ZAP, CLANK!

The next thing I knew, I arrived back home.

"Boy, am I glad to be here!" I said.

"How was it?" Daniel asked me.

"Let's put it this way—there's no time like now!" I said.

I got home just in time for dinner.